INFORMATION

Dedicated to all the Unwanted, lonely, hurt, sad, hungry, cold and abused children in the world.
Know that you are loved very, very much, by all the Animals, Archangels, Angels, Jesus, God Creator and some decent human beings.
We love you more than you could possibly know.
We are fighting for you and we will never, ever, give up.

Copyright © 2021 by Natasha Charlton
Published by www.lulu.com

First paperback edition June 2021

Book design by Natasha Charlton
With special thanks to www.unsplash.com

ISBN 978-1-2913-0351-3
www.mindthebox.co.uk

CONTENTS

Salutations Parents,

Letter writing is a wonderful activity as well as being an essential life skill. Handwritten letters can turn a grey day sunny and bring a warm hug in an envelope. Letter writing can improve a person's communication, social and handwriting skills enormously, as well as encouraging good and healthy manners.

Letter writing, for me, has always been appealing, ever since I was a small child. The fun and excitement of sending or receiving a handwritten letter, showing care and consideration for any special relationship, as well as knowing someone has taken the time to think about the personal connection, is truly divine!

Animals are so friendly and empathic, I just love the idea of writing to them. As a very anxious child, I found it comforting and therapeutic to share my hopes and dreams, even my worries, with my favourite animals, things I might not feel confident enough to say to other human beings.

To help encourage the children to write their own replies, or to send their own letters to loved ones, I have included some templates, hints and tips and checklists and ideas at the back of the book.

This is why I have written this book, to encourage children to write letters, to share their hopes and dreams, to encourage writing skills and to improve personal communication in a technological world

Sincerely,

THE AUTHOR

Dear Loving Child

How wonderful to meet you here!
My name is Lilly Ladybird and I live within the bright and colourful flowers in the park. Do you like to smell the pretty flowers in here too? I'm sure you like to play on the swings more though!

I have a very special job and that is to bring children like you happiness and blessings. This is such fun work. I love it when I see them receive gifts and wonderful things that they deserve. What gifts do you think you deserve?

Call on me to bring a breath of fresh air into your life. Look to me when you feel things are gloomy and I will always be your most trusted friend. Do you have a lucky charm? I would love to be yours.

Sincerely,

MRS LILLY LADYBIRD

From the official desk of
ELEKTRA EAGLE

Hello dearest Child,

Salutations my child of wonder. How wonderful to speak to you in this letter. I am so excited to be able to bring you these words of inspiration. I love to see you happy especially when you are feeling confident and strong.

Strength comes in many ways. Even when we feel small and weak, we can be strong in our hearts. I live on a ledge on a mountain, it has the most amazing views. What can you see when you look out your windows? Do you like to dream of happy things and work hard to make them come true? I can help you with this work, it is part of my spirit job as an Eagle.

Call on me when you feel fragile and I will bring you strength to reach heights you never knew possible. I will nurture you under the care of my strong loving wings. I will help guide and protect you in your dreams too.

Sincerely,

MISS ELEKTRA EAGLE

From the official desk of
STACEY SHEEP

Baaaaaaa. Welcome!

My name is. Stacey Sheep, what's your name? It is lovely to be able to write to you about all of the wonderful things I can help you with. I live in Farmer Willis West Field and there are 18 other sheep here. It is only a small farm but it's my home. My favourite part of the day is when we get schoolchildren to visit and feed us. Their smiles brighten our day so much! Have you ever fed a baby sheep with a bottle?

My spirit job is to help you get in touch with the softer side of yourself. I can help you find feelings of gentleness and kindness towards yourself. Sometimes we find it hard to achieve the things we really want to and we blame ourselves. Well, I'm here to show you that it's ok to be kind to yourself and that is much better than to keep hurting inside.

Call on me to help nurture and love yourself more. Please realise it's OK to feel not so strong and powerful at all times. You may even find me in your dreams bleating about taking care of yourself, which is a most necessary reminder.

Sincerely,

MS STACEY SHEEP

From the official desk of
OLIVER PEACOCK

Dear Loving Child

My name is Oliver Peacock and I live in the Majestic Gardens. The gardens are so pretty all year round, but not quite as pretty as my feathers. My beautiful spirit child, how delightful to be able to write to you and tell you of all the beauty I find in the world. Have you seen a peacock feather? What colour is your favourite feathers? I'm sure I have that colour in my tail!

I do like to show off my pretty tail. However, I am sure to remember to balance beauty with kindness. I like to remember this by telling people that all humans and animals are equal.

Call on me when you feel out of balance and unsettled, I will fondly show you how to build a strong settled feeling within to grow from. If you manage to catch sight of me in a dream, it is a sign of very good luck for you as well.

Sincerely,

MR OLIVER PEACOCK

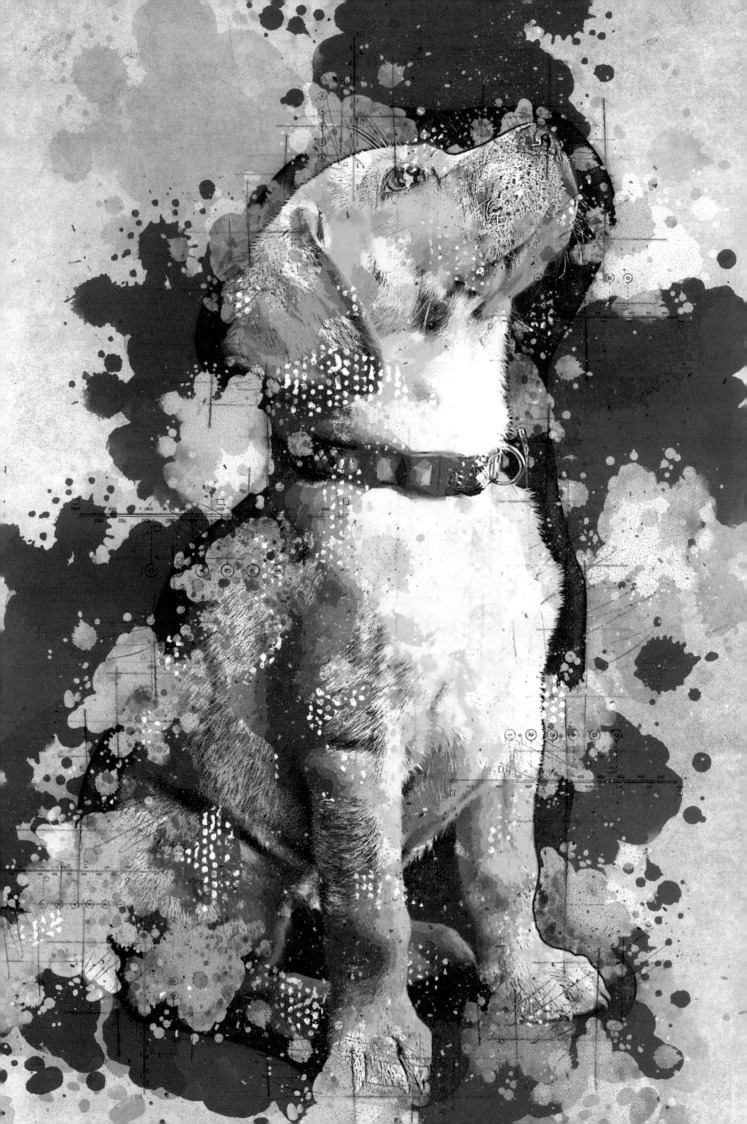

Woof... hello friend,

I'm so excited to write to you. My tail is wagging very hard, it always does that when I'm happy. What do you do when you're excited? I live with my human friends in their house. They are so loving and kind to me, it's brilliant to live here. Do you like where you live?

My spirit job is to bring unconditional love and protection to humans. I love to visit people I care about and let them cuddle me till they feel better. Even when children are not well I can sense this and help them.

I enjoy coming into people's lives to show them what a big heart they have and how much love they have to give. Sometimes they are sad and need reminding of this.

Call on me if you need reminding of how loved and how special you are in the world. I will be there with a wagging tail for you always.

Sincerely,

MR GEORGIE DOG

Dear Loving Child

Little Cub, I am delighted to be able to write to you. I hope this letter finds you well and smiling! My name is Johnny Wolf and I live in the forests of Canada with my Wolf Pack. It's cold and snows a lot here but we love playing in nature and have thick fur coats to keep us warm.
Do you like to play in the Snow?

I am pleased to see you have been using your heart to guide you in difficult situations. My job is to help you trust yourself through the hard times. I like to show you how to follow your own inner guidance. I love to show you your true self. People don't always understand how wonderful that looks to us. What's the most beautiful thing you have ever seen? That doesn't even compare to how beautiful your true self is!

I can also visit you in your dreams and help keep your spirit alive when things may seem down. So, just call on me and I will be there to guide you back to your true spirit self.

Sincerely,

MR JOHNNY WOLF

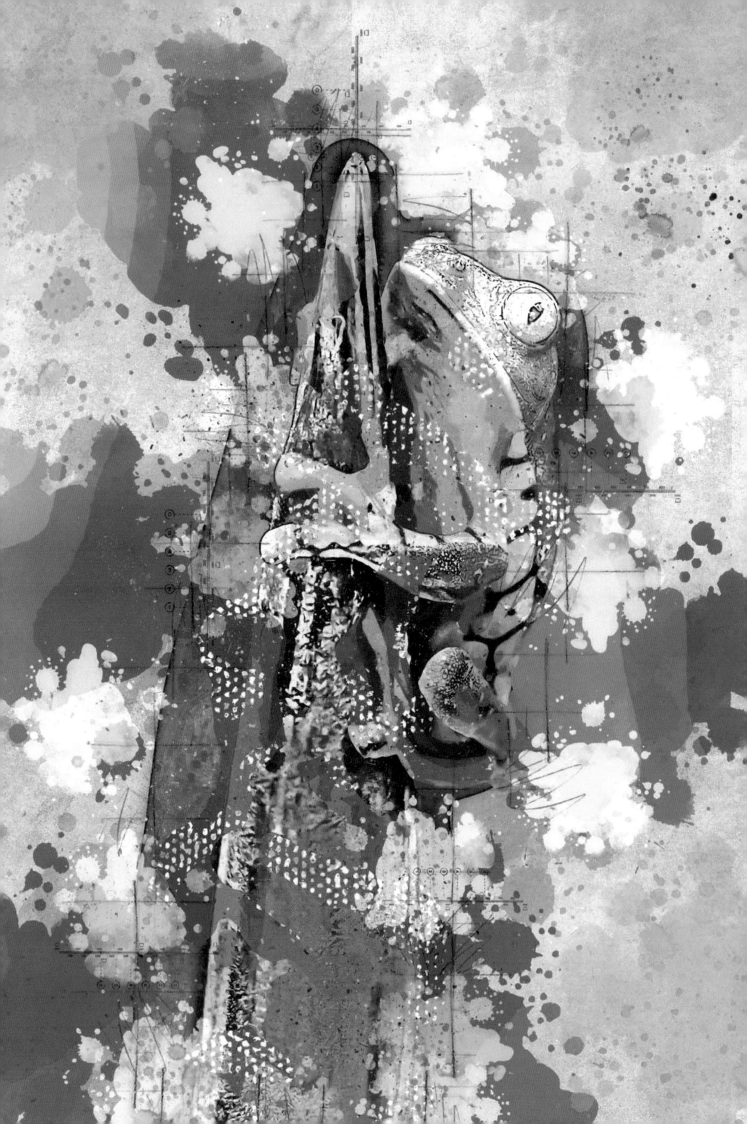

From the official desk of
GERALD FROG

Ribbit!!! Hello.

How wonderful to meet you dearest child. I live in Mrs Smith's Garden pond with 3 gnomes, 7 sparrows and a rather large snail called Percy. Do you have a pond or water feature near you that you like to visit? Do you notice all the life around the pond?

We love to have nice children visit us here. It makes us all happy and celebrate when they smile at us too. I love to splash and hop around the water and onto lilies. The water is so cleansing and refreshing. Do you like splashing too?

My spirit job is to help lift you up when you feel unhappy. I can help clear your horrible feelings away. I can cleanse your sad emotions so that you have room again for all the happy ones that you deserve to feel. Call on me anytime and I will hop into your life to help wash away the dark clouds. Maybe I can even make a triple splash or two in a puddle to put that smile back again!

Sincerely,

MR GERALD FROG

Dear Loving Child

It is so nice to write to you. I have been looking forward to you reading my letter. I was hoping that it would bring you a cheer!

I live in a hollow tree trunk next to the old woods. I love to fly around and bring people messages of wisdom. Do you like to send messages to loved ones too? I did hear from a little field mouse you are very wise, sometimes you are even more clever than the grown ups. Are your grown ups silly sometimes too? I also have a very important job when I visit people. I tell people about changes and the good things that it brings. I know change can be scary and unknown, but it can also be exciting and wonderful.

Please call on me if you are ever worried about changes and I will show you all the beautiful magic that the world has for you to explore.

Sincerely,

MR BENNIE OWL

From the official desk of
JACKIE DEER

Dear Loving Child

I hope this letter finds you happy, I'm so thrilled to write to you here. My name is Jackie Deer and I live in the Caledonian Pine Forests in Scotland. The air and water are so pure and clean here, it's almost untouched by humans. There are not many people who live around here. I do catch a glimpse of one or two pure hearts walking around being at one with nature. This makes me happy we are able to share our world so nicely with each other. Which part of the world would you love to visit?

I am so happy to see your inner light shine bright. You have a big heart that guides others through the darkness. I am proud of how you help other humans too. I like to help you to be loving to yourself when you put so many other people's needs first. Sometimes we forget to recharge our own energy because we are so busy helping others.

I will always be here to remind you to be compassionate and kind and caring to yourself as well as others. You are just as important as anyone else on this planet! Even if I have to come and visit your dreams to remind you, keep an eye out!

Sincerely,

MRS JACKIE DEER

From the official desk of
LUCY SWAN

Greetings and salutations.

My name is Lucy Swan and I'm almost fully grown up just like you! I hope you are feeling well. I can imagine seeing you smile while you read this letter. I love to float around the lakes in parks and watch humans. Sometimes they try to get into boats and end up falling in the water. This makes me giggle so much! As long as I know they are ok, there is no harm done. What funny things do adults do that you like to laugh at?

My job is to show you your true beauty within. I like to teach through songs and poems. Do you have a favourite song?

Sometimes we come across arguments or nasty words which are not pretty. Although this may be upsetting, I can help you deal with these emotions and feel better. Call on me to help you spread your wings and fly free. Let me guide you to form lasting friendships by seeing other people's inner beauty too.

Sincerely,

MS LUCY SWAN

Dear Loving Child

How are you doing? I hope you're fine. My name is Sarah Rabbit and I am so pleased to meet you! I live in a Rabbit Warren inside the earth. It is by an old Oak Tree in Farmer John's Field, with 17 other Rabbits who live there too. I could name them all, but it would take all day. Who do you live with?

I love to eat Carrots and Lettuce left by friendly humans. To receive a warm loving smile is my favourite gift of all! What do you like to be given as a present?

My spirit job is to listen to your worries and sad thoughts and to carry them away. I love to bring you reminders of happy thoughts and wonderful memories. Please talk to me when you feel sad and remember I am always very near to help you smile again.

P.s. I hope you enjoy eating your carrots as well?

Sincerely,

MS SARAH RABBIT

Hello young cub.

I would like to introduce myself. My name is Harry Tiger and I live in Africa, in the open and wild plains. Do not be afraid of my power. I only reflect that of your own strength. It is becoming difficult to live here with the poachers. I like to remember Nature always wins! Is there anything you don't like about where you live? Where would you most like to live if you could choose anywhere?

I have noticed that you have used your own personal courage and determination recently, it has made me so very proud of you. You would be an excellent Tiger!

I really enjoy getting to write to you about my job which is to guide people to find their own will power and inner strength whilst overcoming difficult situations. Call on me anytime when you feel things get too much. Remember me, especially in hard times and I will only be a leap away. Lean on me and feel my power and strength reflect onto yours and we can walk together through anything.

Sincerely,

SIR HARRY TIGER

From the official desk of
FREDDIE FOX

Dear Loving Child

Greetings child, It's lovely to be able to to speak to you in this letter. I live in the woods, but sometimes I sneak into the town at night when there are no humans awake. I do like the bright lights, but home by the trees is where I love to be most. Where is your favourite place to be? Do you like bright lights at night as well?

I can't wait to tell you about my job. I like to work mostly at night and will come and visit you in your dreams. My job is to help bring you ideas and answers when you face problems. I'm very good at thinking and being smart about problems. Do you enjoy doing puzzles?

I can help you with laughter and jokes to raise your spirits if you need some encouragement. I can also help you to be smart about the lessons you learn in life. Call on me if you are ever in a tricky situation and need a different solution, or just for some good fun and laughter.

Sincerely,

MASTER FREDDIE FOX

From the official desk of
GREGORY WHALE

Splash Splash and hello!

I hope this letter finds you well and with a golden smile. How are you feeling today? Do you check in on how you are feeling every day? I hope you do, it's a very important job to remember to do this.

I live in the oceans travelling around with my family and friends. Do you have friends and family that you enjoy travelling with? We get to see happy humans travelling on boats with their loved ones. When they smile at us, if they are good hearted, we sometimes put a show on for them. We can communicate and connect with other whales over thousands of miles of ocean.

I love to visit you in dreams and show you how to be more confident inside, so that you can achieve your personal goals. My job is to help you understand talking with your inner self, which in turn helps to bridge gaps in communicating with others. Sometimes these gaps can feel so big that we are unable to reach people we love. Fear not, it is not impossible with me by your side. Together, we can achieve all you wish to seek, through understanding ourselves better first.

Sincerely,

MR GREGORY WHALE

Greetings from the Far East!

I am writing all the way from China to encourage and help you. My name is Jamie Panda and I live amongst the bamboo and tropical forests. I love to eat Bamboo, but most of all I love to see happy smiling people! What foods do you like to eat?

I am a very sensitive animal and can sense my surroundings very well. This can be hard sometimes if I don't feel comfortable where I am. I have many ways to deal with these feelings and would love to share them with you. What are you feeling right now? Where are you reading this, is it a place that you like?

My job is to guide you to make happy spaces and set boundaries so that you may feel safe and secure in the world. Call on me when you feel uncomfortable and uneasy, and I will help nurture you back into a loving place where you feel comfortable. I love to cuddle and cherish you in your dreams, so look out for me there too!

Sincerely,

MR JAMIE PANDA

Dear Loving Child

I hope this letter finds you well and in peace, dear child. My name is Helen Turtle and I live in the beautiful tropical islands of the Indian Ocean. I live here with the Whales and Dolphins and all sorts of wonderful sea life. I find it ever so peaceful swimming and floating and splashing.

I like to take my time and walk slowly though my journey. Do you know why turtles walk slow? It's so we can get to take in all the magic we pass by everyday. By slowing down a little you will get to notice the magic much more too. Why don't you try it?

My job is to help you to find an easier pace of life. This really helps when it gets too hectic. I can help you keep calm and walk in peace through any troubles you may run into. Call on me when you are faced with tough decisions or situations. I will lovingly guide you to the most thoughtful ideas and answers in calm and peaceful ways. Being slower sometimes does have its advantages, just remember to tell the Hare next time you see him!

Sincerely,

MS HELEN TURTLE

From the official desk of
DONALD HORSE

Hello Neighbour!

My name is Donald Horse and I live in the nice warm stables up on the hill, by the Manor House. Do you live on a hill? It's much more fun going down the hill than up a hill, I must agree. I like to motivate humans to do tasks that are not so much fun, such as doing chores or even moving house. Let me be your strength and driving force when you feel empty and powerless to finish your difficult tasks. What is the hardest thing you have ever done?

I love to watch you smile after you finish your tasks with the energy of determination. I am very proud of you for climbing up that hill with your inner strength. Whenever you feel unable to complete your goals, call on me always! We will walk up the hill together, so we can have all the fun of running back down with the wind in our Maine and feel like we are flying.

I look forward to seeing you there.

Sincerely,

MR DONALD HORSE

From the official desk of
DANNY DOLPHIN

Greetings from the Ocean!

I love to see happy children splashing about in water and having fun. I get to do it all day long too! Do you like bubble baths? I don't get to have baths in the ocean as the bubbles are not good for us like they are for you.

I like to spend a lot of time living peacefully in the ocean with lots and lots of other animal species, we get along so well. Do you live with any other animals or pets? We are very gentle animals and love to play around with kind humans and their boats.

Sometimes we get upset at other people, and it's natural to feel like this sometimes too. My job as Dolphin is to bring peace and calm and understanding. Come and call on me to play with and I will remind you how to look for the good in everyone and restore your inner peace and calm. I hope you never feel lonely either. I will always be here for you to play with, even in your dreams.

Sincerely,

MASTER DANNY DOLPHIN

APPENDIX

HINTS AND TIPS FOR WRITING LETTERS

- **Headings:** This can include adding your contact details for a reply and the date you write the letter. This usually goes in the top right hand corner of the page.

- **Greetings:** This is where you say hello to the recipient. You can use a variety of greetings based on formal or informal communication. Also remember to Include a comma after this line.

- **Explain yourself:** You can start by writing an explanation of why you have decided to write the letter. If you have written to them many times you can thank them for their last letter. If you do not know someone that well, you can say how you met them or know them.

- **Ask me something:** This is a really friendly way to connect with someone at the start and turn it into a longer conversation.

- **What is the news?** Try and add some good news. This is a really good place to add something happy that has happened recently or sharing any plans for the future.

- **Keep it interesting:** This is a great way to add any good facts, information or jolly jokes that you would like to share. Maybe even a book or movie recommendation?

- **Answers please!** Do not forget to answer any questions you may have been asked before if this is not your first time writing to them. This is a great way to share things, gain a deeper relationship with the reader and keep the letters flowing.

- **Last but not least:** You can add some personal wishes here. Don't forget to end with something positive and encourage them to write back to you.

- **Who wrote this?** The final part of the letter is to add your name and an good closing sentence, keeping in mind is it to a friend or a new person?

- **P.S.** This is short for "Postscript" and here you can add anything you forgot without having to write the whole letter again.

IDEAS TO WRITE ABOUT IN YOUR LETTERS

1. Do you have any pets? What do you like about them?
2. What do you like about your home?
3. Is there anything interesting you are learning about at the moment?
4. Where is your favourite place to go in your hometown?
5. What is your favourite food?
6. What is your best joke that you like to share with your friends?
7. Do you have any family traditions?
8. Which season is your favourite?
9. Has anything interesting happened to you recently?
10. Have you been to any exciting places on your holidays?
11. Where was the last place you went to on a day trip?
12. Have you read any good books recently? Would you recommend them?
13. What is your favourite colour? How does it make you feel?
14. Do you enjoy any sports? What is your favourite team?
15. What is your favourite movie/book character? Why do you like them?
16. What achievement are you most proud of in your life?
17. What did you do recently that really helped another person?
18. What gift did you get recently? What did you think about it?
19. What would be your ideal job in the future? Why do you like it?
20. Has anything funny happened to you lately?
21. What are you grateful for in your life right now?
22. Do you have a nickname? If not, what name would you choose?
23. What superpower would you like to have the most?
24. If you could be an animal for a day, which one would you be?
25. Do you like to do any arts and crafts? What did you last make?
26. Do you have a hobby? How often do you get to do it?
27. Have you ever met a famous person? What were they like?
28. What music do you like? Who is your favourite musician and why?
29. How many people are in your family and what are they like?
30. Is there any place in the world you would like to visit and why?

LETTER WRITING CHECKLIST

- [ ] Have you Included contact details for replies
- [ ] Have you added the date the letter was written
- [ ] Did you start with a greeting - Don't forget the Comma after!
- [ ] Did you Introduce yourself? - If you haven't written before
- [ ] Did you thank them for their letter? - If you are replying to them
- [ ] Is it a friendly or formal letter? Do your words show this?
- [ ] Have you answered any questions that they asked if replying?
- [ ] Have you asked them any questions?
- [ ] Have you checked your spelling and punctuation?
- [ ] Did you remember to add some fun information?
- [ ] Have you put the letter into paragraph sections?
- [ ] Did you add a friendly ending?
- [ ] Did you add your name at the bottom?
- [ ] Did you make sure to not make it too long?
- [ ] Did you make sure you put everything you wanted to say?
- [ ] Did you read the letter over to make sure you are happy with it?
- [ ] If you forgot anything, did you add a P.S at the bottom?

HELLO

TO
_____
_____
_____
_____

PLEASE WRITE BACK TO ME HERE:
....
....
....
....

A PICTURE FOR YOU

SOMETHING FUN I DID THIS WEEK WAS:
....
....
....
....
....

TODAY'S DATE IS:

MY FAVOURITE THINGS ARE

I WOULD LIKE TO ASK YOU...

?

Best Wishes

FROM
....

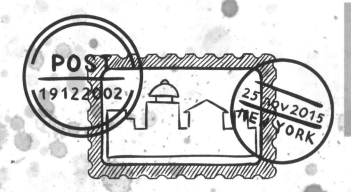

POST
19122002
25 NOV 2015
NEW YORK

ADDRESS:

DATE:

DEAR

I AM WRITING TO SAY:

I HAVE ENJOYED:

TODAY I FEEL:

SOMETHING INTERESTING I FOUND OUT WAS:

I WOULD LIKE TO ASK YOU:

BEST WISHES,

FROM:

Printed in Great Britain
by Amazon

18467391R00029